Books in the Linkers series

Homes discovered through Art & Technology
Homes discovered through Geography
Homes discovered through History
Homes discovered through Science

Toys discovered through Art & Technology
Toys discovered through Geography
Toys discovered through History
Toys discovered through Science

Myself discovered through Art & Technology
Myself discovered through Geography
Myself discovered through History
Myself discovered through Science

Water discovered through Art & Technology
Water discovered through Geography
Water discovered through History
Water discovered through Science

First paperback edition 1996
First published 1996 in hardback by A&C Black (Publishers) Limited
35 Bedford Row, London WC1R 4JH

ISBN 0-7136-4583-0
A CIP catalogue record for this book is available from the British Library.

Copyright © 1996 BryantMole Books

Commissioned photographs by Zul Mukhida
Design by Jean Wheeler   Picture research by Liz Harman

Consultants: Grant Jones, Art Adviser, E. Sussex
Ian Punter, Adviser in Design Technology, E. Sussex

The publishers would like to thank the children of Northiam C. E. School, East Sussex,
who worked so hard to produce the artwork featured in this book, and Judy Grahame who
facilitated and guided its production.

Acknowledgements

Lesley and Roy Adkins; 6, Bridgeman Art Library; Wallace Collection, London 16, Johnny van Haeften Gallery, London 17
(left), Chapel Studios; 22 (both), Eye Ubiquitious; 10 (left), 12 (right), Harlequin; 14 (left), Positive Images; 4 (both), 7 (left),
Tony Stone; Derek Kartum 2, Paul Rees 3 (left), Steven Peters 3 (right), Jon Riley 8 (right), Visual Arts Library; Washington
Terra Museum of American Art 17 (right), Zefa; 7 (right).

Printed and bound in Italy by L.E.G.O.

Homes

discovered through
Art and Technology

Karen Bryant-Mole

Contents

A & C Black • London

Homes

Homes are places where people live.
Homes come in all shapes and sizes.
They are made from different things.

Homes have to be designed and then
they have to be built.
How would you describe your home?

Once a home has been built,
it is decorated.
The wallpaper, the carpets, the
curtains and even the colour of
the paint have to be designed
by someone and then made.

Finally, we put furniture into our homes.
Furniture, too, has to be designed
and made.
There are lots of different styles of
furniture, available in many different
colours and materials, so that people can
choose the furniture that they prefer.

Old and new

The home below was designed and built about five hundred years ago. It was built around a frame made from wood.

This home was only built about twenty years ago. What differences can you see between this house and the older house?

What sort of home
would you choose
to live in?
You could make
a picture of your
dream home.

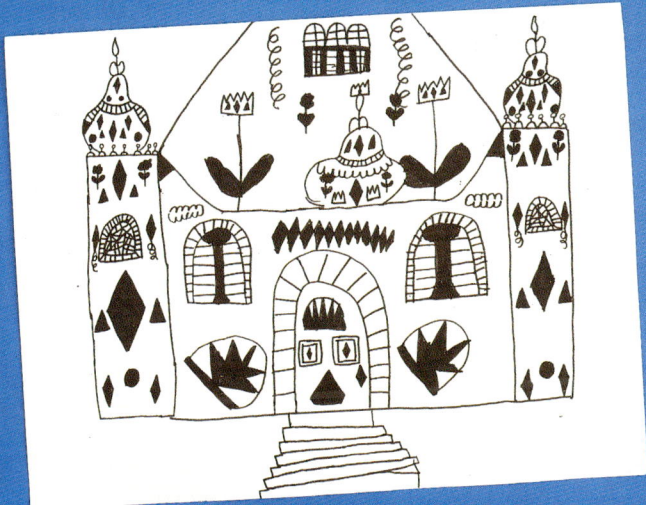

Here are some ideas for homes.
Which do you prefer?
Why?

Homes as art

Homes are designed by architects.
An architect is a type of artist.

Architects have been designing
buildings for many thousands
of years.
Different styles of architecture
have different names.

This large house is
almost 300 years old.
It is built in the
Baroque style.

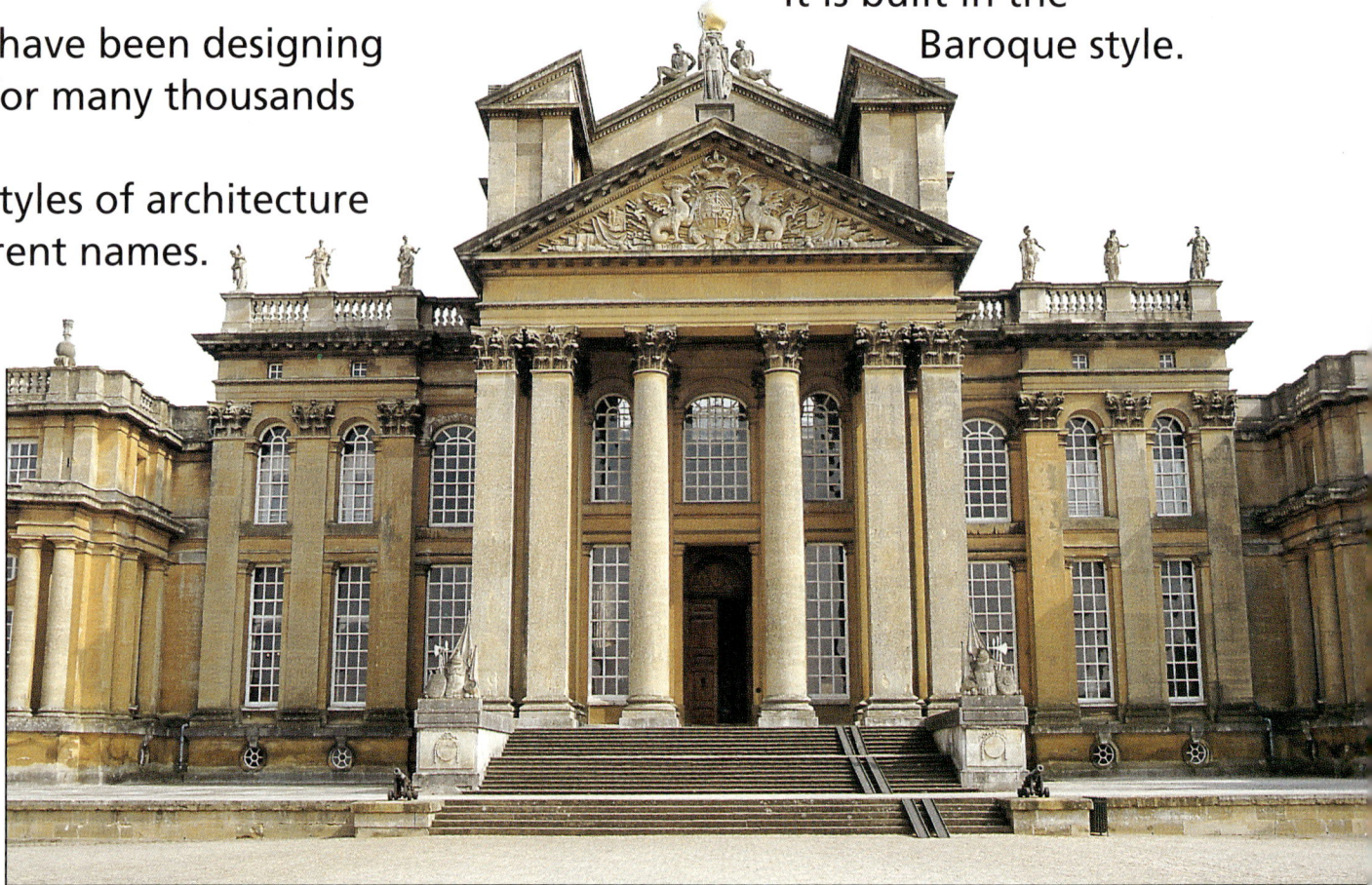

The picture below shows part of a row of Regency homes. They were built nearly 200 years ago.

The flats above were built about 60 years ago.
They were built in a style that is known as Bauhaus.

Why not find out more about different styles of architecture?

Design

Architects make sketches of the building they are designing.
Then they draw up plans.
The people in the picture on the right are looking at a set of floor plans.
Floor plans are drawings that show the size and shape of the rooms and the position of the doors and windows.

You could draw up a floor plan for your dream home.
You will need some squared paper, a ruler, a pencil, a rubber and a pen.

Think about the number of rooms you want and what they will be used for. Here are some finished floor plans.

This home has all the rooms on one floor.

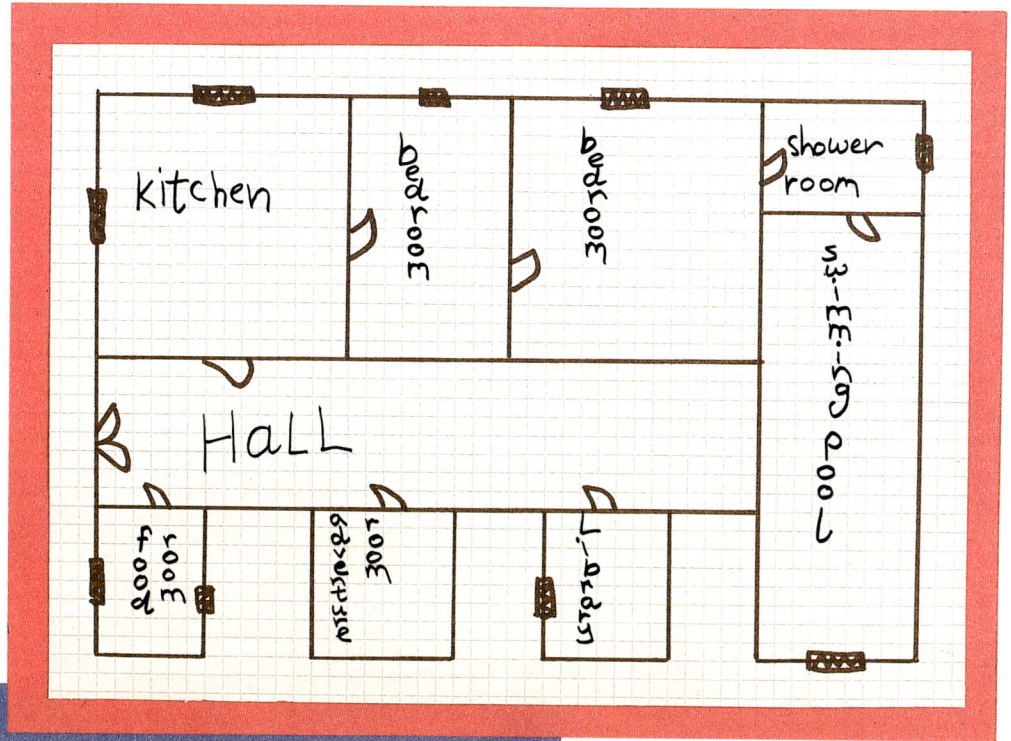

Plan 1 (one floor):
- kitchen
- bedroom
- bedroom
- shower room
- swimming pool
- HaLL
- food room
- exercise room
- library

Plan 2 (two floors):
- Play room
- Ice rink
- kitchen
- Pets room
- Sun room
- Bath room
- Bed Room
- Cinema
- Jacuzzi room

This home has two floors, or storeys.

Models

It can be hard to imagine what a building will look like from a plan.
This model of a new housing estate has been built so that people can see what it will look like in real life.

Why not make a model of part of the street that you live in?

Or you could make a model of an imaginary street.

You could make your model from small, empty boxes and other things that people have finished using.

A group of children have made this street scene.
Can you see the street lights?
They have been made from straws and paper.

Building

These builders are building a new house. They have to lay the bricks, put in the windows and doors and put on the roof.

The things they use to make the house are called construction materials. Construction means building.

These toys are called construction toys.
You can use them to build lots of different things.
There are many types of construction toy.

Here are some homes
that have been built using
construction toys.
Why not try this yourself?

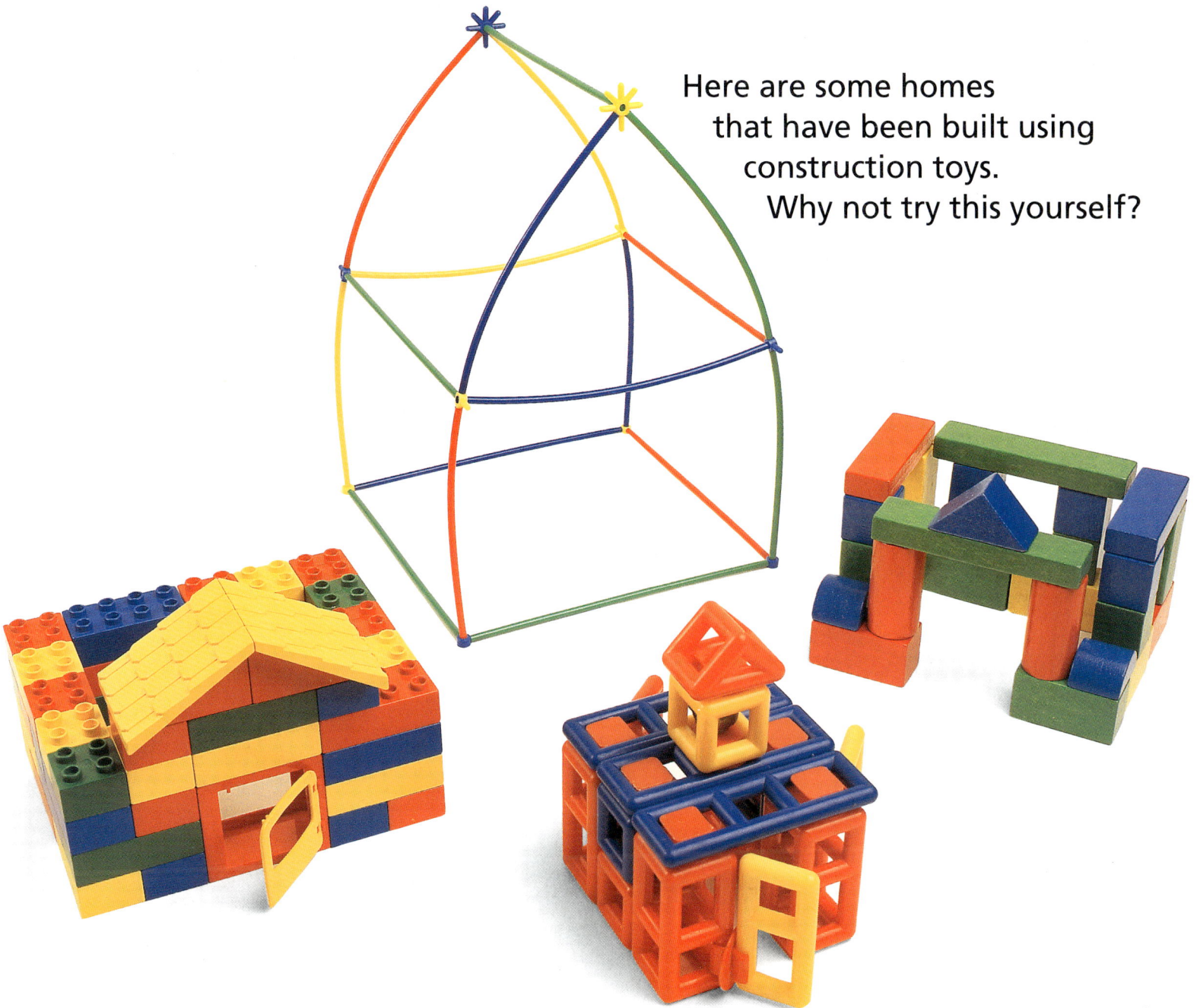

Wallpaper

The walls in the room below have been decorated in patterned wallpaper.
The wallpaper has a flower pattern that is repeated over and over again.
The pattern has been printed onto the wallpaper.

To print your own wallpaper you need some paper, some paint and something that will make an interesting print.
Objects like cotton reels, plastic bricks and pieces of wood make good designs.
Make sure you check with an adult before you put paint on anything.

Here are some strips of wallpaper that have been designed and printed by children.

Can you spot a print that was made by using string pressed into a lump of Plasticine?

Homes in art

Throughout the years, artists have painted pictures of people in their homes.

This picture was painted about 350 years ago.

Paintings can show us the type of homes that people lived in.

The picture below was also painted about 350 years ago.
Paintings of homes can tell us about the people who lived in them.
We can see that the family who lived here was much poorer than the family in the picture on the left.

This family had their picture painted outdoors.
As well as seeing the family, we can also see what their garden looked like.

Keep a look out for homes in other works of art.

Pictures

Many people like to hang pictures in their homes.
Pictures usually have frames around them.
Picture frames are designed to show off the picture and make it look special.

You could make your own picture frame. You will need some strips of card for the base of the frame and some odds and ends to decorate it.

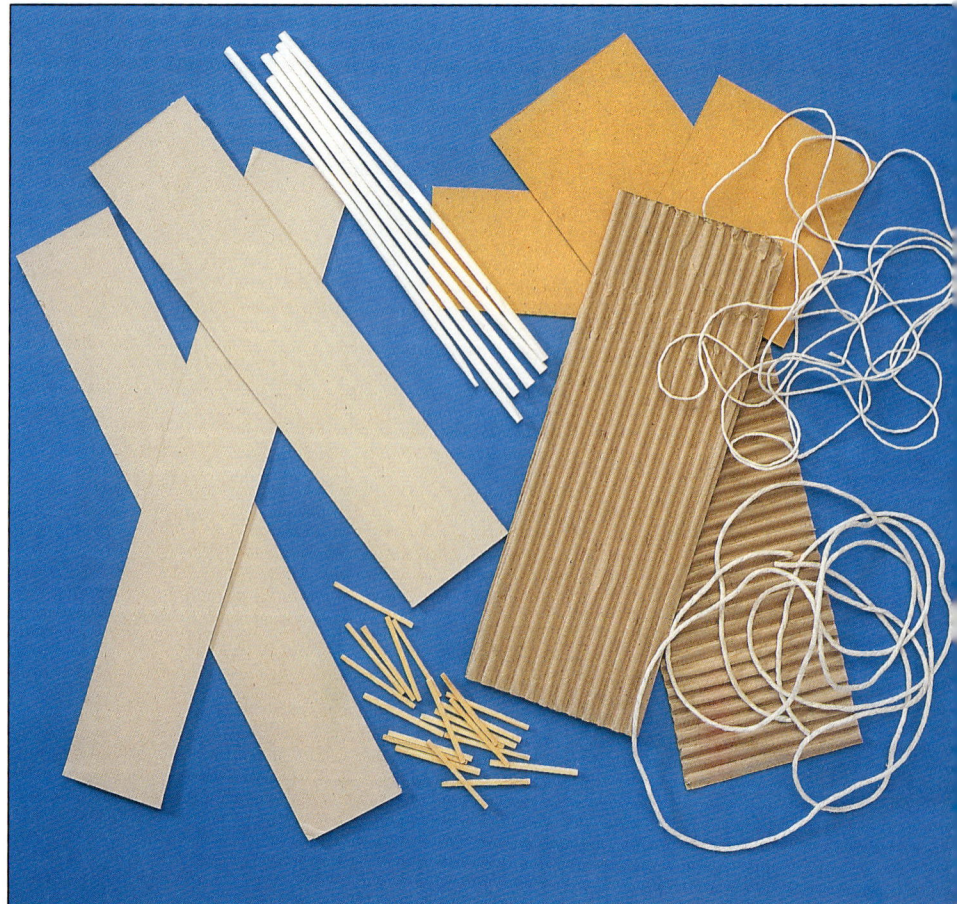

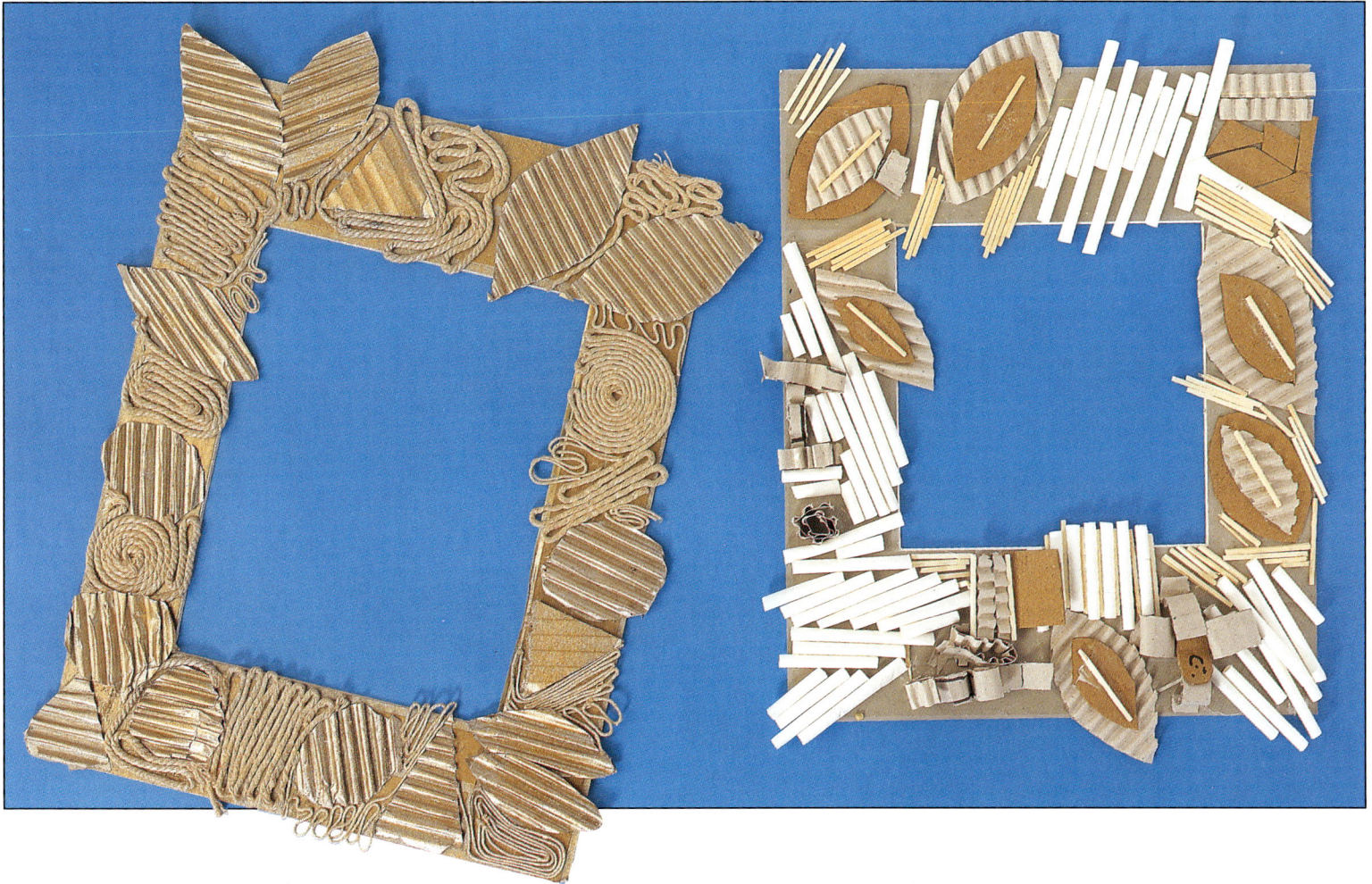

What do you think of these frames? One of the frames has been painted.

As well as being used for pictures, these frames could be used as photo frames or even mirror frames.

Clay

Lots of things around our homes are made from clay.
Bowls, cups, vases and ornaments are often made from clay.
Washbasins and tiles are made from clay, too.

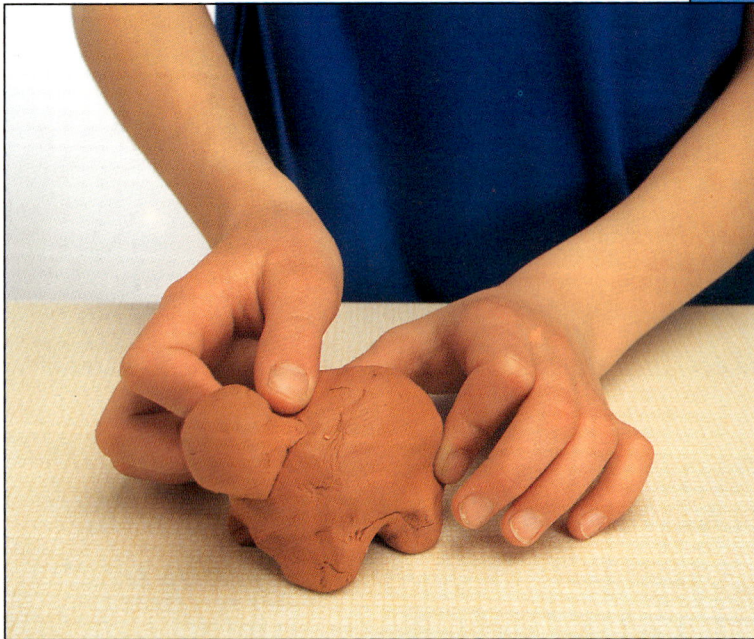

Clay can be pulled and pushed and pinched into all sorts of shapes.

It can be rolled into long sausages and then coiled around.

Why not use clay to make something to decorate your bedroom?
Which of these ornaments do you like best?

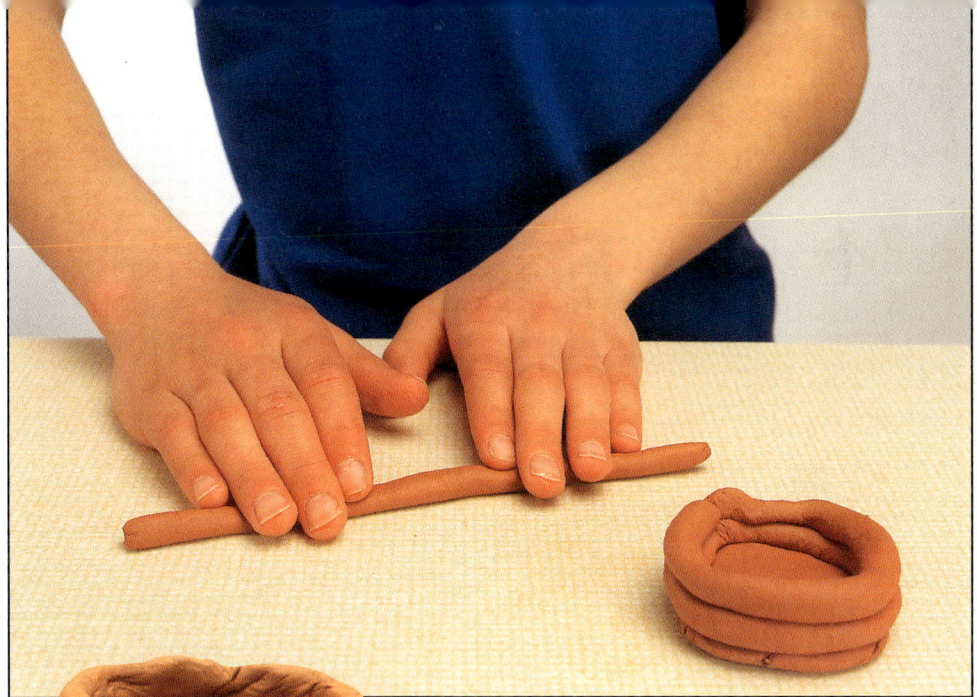

Machines

Many of the machines around our homes have been invented to make our lives easier, and to help us get jobs done quickly.

Before vacuum cleaners were invented, floors had to be brushed and carpets had to be shaken outside.

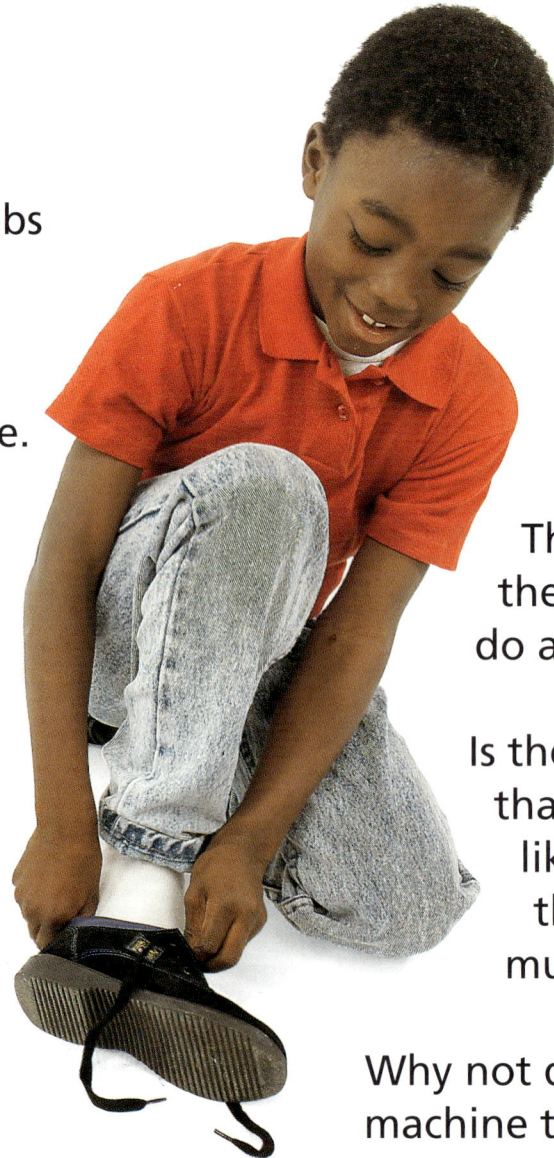

Think of all the things you do at home.

Is there anything that you don't like doing or that takes too much time?

Why not design a machine to help you?

Here are some finished designs.
Can you find a machine that tidies
bedrooms, a machine that does
the washing up and a machine
that gets you dressed?

Glossary

architecture the way in which a building is designed and built
clay a special type of earth
designed planned
housing estate a group of homes, usually built at the same time
imaginary make-believe, pretend

invent make or think of something new
materials what things are made from
ornaments decorations
position where something is
sketches rough drawings

Index

How to use this book

Each book in this series takes a familiar topic or theme and focuses on one area of the curriculum: science, art and technology, geography or history. The books are intended as starting points, illustrating some of the many different angles from which a topic can be studied. They should act as springboards for further investigation, activity or information seeking.

The following list of books may prove useful.

Further books to read

Series	Title	Author	Publisher
Design and Make	Houses and Homes	J. Williams	Wayland
First Arts and Crafts	Painting Printing Models	S. Stocks	Wayland
First Skills	Starting Drawing Starting Painting	S. Mayes	Usborne
Get Set Go!	all Craft Activity titles	R. Thomson	Watts
How to Draw	How to Draw Buildings	P. Beasant	Usborne
Jump! Starts Crafts	Models	I. Bulloch	Watts
Painting and Drawing	all titles	M. Comellia	A&C Black